BETTER SERVED HOT

EROTIC SHORT STORY

HEATHER STOLTS

plicit Press
Erotica Fiction

CHAPTER 1

BRIANA

BRIANNA WOKE up with a sense of dread. Her cat leaped on the bed and mewed insistently. She knew Brianna was awake, so there was no avoiding the day. She reached for her phone. On the screen was the blinking reminder of the day's tasks. She almost crawled back into bed to hide.

Today was her first day at her new job.

It was the first time in almost three years that she would have to interact with people every day. She wasn't sure she was up to it, but the job was too good to pass up. She had studied and researched in her own lab for years and now was her chance to see if her research had practical applications. Besides, after all those years in the lab, she needed to make some money. It didn't matter how much she hated it. She had to do it.

She unenthusiastically crawled out of bed and went to the closet. She was very organized and her clothes were hung neatly by color. She selected a plain white blouse and a pair of slim black pants. Pants were practical for lab work. This was the first day; she might not be spending the day in the lab or even see it right away. She sighed, put the pants back, and pulled out one of her two skirts.

She quickly showered and applied light makeup. Normally she wouldn't have bothered, but her red hair came with light eyebrows and eyelashes. Her natural look wouldn't translate well in the business world.

She spent so much time applying the unfamiliar make-up that she didn't have time to worry about her hair. She simply pulled it back with a band, not realizing that with her simple outfit and light make-up she looked more like a young college student than a consultant for one of the top corporations in the country.

A quick cup of coffee and a pat on the cat's head later and she was out the door.

She left in plenty of time to get to the building, but she hadn't planned on parking. She circled the building at least three times before finally calling the office. She was directed to the executive parking and was a little shocked to discover that she was considered an executive. She pushed her shock back down when she noticed that she was running late.

She pulled in and was about to pull into a space when she was deafened by a loud honking sound. A bright sports car zipped in front of her and into the space. She was so stunned she simply sat in her car for a moment. She quickly found another spot and parked, focused on the time. She walked as quickly as she could her long stride hampered by the skirt. She noticed that the skirt was shorter than she remembered. She didn't have time to worry about that. She had only a few minutes to get to her first meeting.

As she step-hopped down the hall she stumbled a bit. She was caught by a firm, sure hand. She looked up and couldn't believe her eyes. She was staring into a very famil-iar, very handsome face. His dark, smoldering looks had haunted her for almost fifteen years. She could tell by his slick smile that he didn't recognize her. There wasn't even a glimmer of recognition. She gave him a cool look.

"Thank you." With that, she gathered herself and her things and continued down the hall to her office. She hardly had time to reel over the fact that she had an office and that her name and credentials were etched into the glass when she was summoned into a meeting. She quickly grabbed a notebook and found her way to the conference room.

When she walked in, she realized that her wardrobe was in desperate need of updating. Everyone else was also dressed conservatively, but she felt shabby. The other women in the room were glossy in appearance, from their nails to their perfectly coiffed hair. Brianna knew that shiny, pointy nails were impractical in her line of work, but she could certainly smarten up a little. The meeting was called to order and she was introduced to everyone. Everyone and Him. Anthony Pistone. Of course, she knew him as Tony "The Pistol" Pistone. He was the star athlete at her Middle School, then her High School, and probably wherever he went to college. When she knew him, he was the best. Best at everything from lacrosse to tennis, there wasn't any sport he couldn't play. The only thing he couldn't do was math. Or science or anything he couldn't charm his way around.

She wasn't surprised that he didn't recognize her. She was never a blip on his radar years ago. No, she wasn't surprised at all that he didn't remember her. She was surprised that he didn't even look at her when he was introduced. She knew she was plain, but still, she was an executive at this company. Surely that deserved some spark of interest.

After the meeting, she didn't have time to dwell on times past or do much of anything else but try and catch her breath. She raced from office to office getting everyone's notes on the current project. It was almost six o'clock when she entered all of the information into her database. She was hoping for a chance to check out the actual lab, but if she wanted to invest in her wardrobe upgrades, she needed to get moving.

She was very lucky not to have run into Anthony again. To be honest, she didn't know how she would have reacted.

Anthony's day was finally coming to an end. He had been hoping to get a chance to talk to the new girl. He had been called into a conference and was occupied for so long that he was unable to talk to her. He liked the way she looked, not overdone like so many women he met. He really liked the way she didn't react at all to him. He knew he was good-looking. He knew that his good looks and athletic build were major factors in his success. He hadn't met anyone in a long time that seemed immune to it. She was so immune to it that she didn't even give him a second look when he passed her in the lobby on the way to the garage.

Brianna drove to the nearest mall and walked straight

past the large chain department store into a tiny boutique. The one store employee rushed right over and hugged her.

"Oh my God, you left the house. Is it the Apocalypse? Are there zombies?"

"You are not funny."

"I am a little funny; you're just too close to me to appreciate it. So what brings you to the mall?"

"I need clothes."

"Oh, that's right, the new job. I'm sorry your incognito nun-wear didn't pass muster."

"I don't have time to banter. Can you help me or not?"

"Of course, I will, that's what sisters are for. Give me ten minutes."

Brianna walked around the mall to stretch her legs and realized that she had no idea what was happening in the real world anymore. Very few women were in skirts and those that were had skirts barely longer than their panty line. She was no prude, but how did they get anything done? Almost every woman was also wearing heels that made them walk like newborn colts. Maybe she had put off this trip for too long.

She was swept away as soon as she went into the boutique. She was poked and prodded and clothes were draped around her. She didn't know what size she wore so there was some measuring in there. Once her sister had established her size, there was an endless barrage of skirts, dresses, and slim-fitting trousers. She got away without buying shoes by agreeing to come back later in the week for another spree. Just when she thought she could drag her exhausted body home, her sister threw her to the wild pack of cosmetic saleswomen who took one look at her gold card and went crazy. Her skin was buffed and cleansed and toned. Then she was slathered with make-up only to have it removed again. Her sister documented every moment of it, she said she was filming so that Brianna could review the footage to learn how to put the make-up on in the morning, but Brianna thought that it was probably to show at the family reunion.

Exhausted by her day, Brianna thought she could just walk past her computer and go to bed. She couldn't do it. She walked straight over to the desk and booted up. A few keystrokes later and there it was. "Tony the Pistol" proudly riding the float that she and the rest of the science department had worked for hours on. She wondered if things would have turned out any different if she hadn't stopped the intricate practical joke from happening. It didn't matter. Tony proudly paraded through town with a cloud of silvery bubbles floating around him like a halo. He had no concept of the work that went into it, let alone the trouble she went through to keep him from the geyser of bright pink indelible ink that would have rained down on him if she hadn't stopped it.

She smiled at the picture. At the time she had hoped that he would have found out how she had saved him from embarrassment and shame. He would be so moved by the gesture that he would come to find her at the dance and sweep her off her feet and carry her to the center of the dance floor, removing the pencil that held her hair up in its messy bun. She remembered how her heart had skipped and how she had trembled with excitement. This was the point when she turned off the computer. Today, she didn't.

The memory came flooding back over her. She didn't have time to stop it. Suddenly there she was, a very naïve sixteen-year-old; the youngest senior in the whole class. She didn't go to the homecoming dance, but she did go to one of the parties. She was surprised that Tony had stopped by. He was very drunk but she found his stumbling and slightly slurring words charming. She had been lingering near the kitchen, and he saw her there. She was tugging at the edge of her skirt. Her sister had coaxed her into wearing it and she was a little self-conscious about it.

Tony had come over offering her a red cup of beer. She smiled shyly as he said, "I hate to see a pretty girl without a drink." She had been so flattered her mouth went dry and she couldn't think of anything to say. She wanted to say that she didn't remember what happened next, but she did. Vividly. She remembered every single detail. How Tony had slipped his arm around her and drew her outside to the dark porch. She remembered how her heart had skipped a beat when he kissed her softly. She remembered thinking wildly that he had found out how she had saved him from humiliation and that maybe, just maybe he really saw her now and wanted her to be a part of his glorious life. At sixteen she still believed in the knights in shining armor and princes who rescued the girl in rags.

His kisses were soft and slightly sour with the taste of the beer. She kissed him back and their teeth clacked against each other awkwardly. He laughed and kissed her chin then returned to kissing her mouth. His lips worked magic across her chin and he licked and nibbled at her neck. The tingles ran up and down her spine. She moaned softly when he slipped his hand under her shirt. His hand was warm on her stomach and she felt herself shiver. He murmured something about keeping her warm and he wrapped his other arm around her while he stroked her skin. His hand massaged and fondled her breast. Her nipple grew hard against his hand. He dropped his head down and he nipped at her lightly. She moaned.

His hand worked its way between her legs. He

rearranged his position so he could reach her easily. His hand massaged her mound and her legs fell apart to give him access. He placed her hand on his fly. She was amazed and a little frightened by how big and firm he felt. She felt another, different kind of shiver and a growing warmth and wetness between her legs.

His fingers had now slipped under the edge of her panties and were working their way further. She gasped when his fingers stroked her lips lightly, exploring. His kisses grew deeper and more urgent. She jumped slightly when he slid one finger inside her. He twirled it around lightly and kissed her even deeper. He kissed her until she relaxed and he began moving his finger in and out steadily. She moaned again. He kissed her jaw and whispered for her to be a little quieter. She bit her lower lip to suppress any other moans. She felt the wetness between her legs grow and he slipped a second finger into her. It was so quiet outside that she could hear the sound of his fingers moving in and out of her. She had never felt anything as exquisite as this. She wanted to throw back her head and moan. It was getting harder and harder to stay quiet. He speeded up the movement of his fingers. She got wetter and her whole body stiffened up. Suddenly she was swept over with waves of pure electric pleasure. She felt as if she had burst into a million pieces in the most delightful way. The waves were subsiding and she heard his zipper open. She was almost in a trance when he nudged her head downward.

She wasn't completely naïve, she knew what he wanted. After the pleasure he had given her, she wanted to return the favor. She opened her mouth and took him in. His skin was surprisingly smooth. His penis felt like velvet-covered steel. His skin was slightly salty tasting and she gloried in the taste of him. She relished the male smell of him. She didn't know if she should lick or suck so she did both. All she could think about was how to please him. She could always get better. She knew that the intimacy of this act meant they were going to be together. She smiled as she heard him moan. She used his sounds as cues to suck or lick or to slow down. She just wanted to give him the pleasure that he gave her. Finally, he moaned, "Oh Fuck." And then climaxed. The salty fluid wasn't a complete surprise and she swallowed it, not knowing what else to do.

He gave her a pat on the head as he moved away. With that he zipped up his pants and headed back into the party, taking a drink from his beer. She sat outside alone, certain that he was only using the bathroom and would soon be back.

She sat outside for an hour before she went home. She never told anyone what had happened; she just went on about her lonely little high school nerd life.

She clicked off the computer. Tomorrow was going to be a long day. Tomorrow she was going to make sure he remembered her.

She didn't remember falling asleep, but she must have because she woke to the sandpaper tongue of her cat relentlessly licking the side of her face. She was grateful that the insistence of her cat made her wake up early; she wanted the extra time to get ready. She reached for the new steel gray trousers that cupped her ass and made it appear perky. The flat front style made the most of her naturally slender frame. Her stomach looked impossibly flat. With this, she paired a French blue tailored blouse that made her eyes sparkle a dark turquoise. She painted her face lightly, darkening her lashes and brows. She caught her hair back with a clip. She gave herself a pleased look in the mirror and left for work, making a note to call her sister later.

She pulled her car into her assigned space and confidently strode into the building. She had no idea where his office was and she didn't care. She repeated that over and over to herself as she walked to her office. She was able to occupy her mind with a few small things before she went to visit the lab. From what she remembered, he wasn't the scientific type, so no danger of running into him there. She collected her key cards and headed down the hall. She made sure that her walk was confident and sure, but when she got to the lab, she fumbled and dropped her cards.

Of course, this was when Tony appeared. He scooped the cards up for her and smiled as he handed them to her. She looked him square in the eye and gave him a cool thank you. She didn't return his smile. She took pride in his puzzled look and she briskly walked into the lab.

Her heart was beating rapidly as she wondered how long this would take.

It only took as long as lunch. She returned to find Tony lurking around her office. She made sure that she didn't show any reaction to his warm smile. She was delighted to see the confusion cross his face. He followed her into her office and she said, "Yes?"

"I know you're new to the company and I was wondering if you needed anything."

"I didn't realize I had an assistant."

She laughed coyly at his flustered look.

"Relax, I'm kidding. You're a little older than the other assistants."

"Actually I'm in marketing."

"Of course you are."

She was very glad that she had taken an extra moment to reapply lipstick; it made her cool bitchy remarks easier to bite out. She had to admit that her sister had been right about the makeover making her feel better.

"Have I done anything to offend you?"

She crossed her office in two strides of her long legs. She stood close enough to him to kiss him. She smiled and said,

"Not today."

His dark eyes locked on to hers. She took a tiny step forward. She felt his hand begin to move up to her waist. The phone rang shrilling them both back to awareness.

As she walked to her desk she dismissed him with an, "If there's nothing else. . ." Tony left without saying anything.

She was almost giddy with the success of this action. She hadn't really planned on doing things this way, but it was better than anything she could have come up with. The rest of the day went by in a flash. She planned meetings around her wardrobe choices as she wrote a glowing report of the lab and its staff. The next few days were a blur of activity. She made sure that she visited every department. Everyone was thoroughly charmed by her. She quickly won over the interns and assistants by looking them in the eye and thanking them by name when they brought copies and coffee to her at meetings.

By the time Tony invited her to a marketing meeting everyone knew who she was. Everyone greeted her with a warm smile. She sat near the front of the conference room. When Tony walked to the front, she crossed her legs. Tony watched her skirt climb up her thigh. She looked up and caught his eye. He had the decency to blush. She knew that he would be watching her hemline for the rest of the meeting. She only had to check once by dropping her pen and scooting it back over to her. Bending over caused her skirt to rise up to the mid thigh.

It wouldn't be long now.

It wasn't. She was in the supply room to get binder clips. That was her excuse. She really went in there because she saw him walking in there. He turned when he heard her walk in. He gave her a tentative smile and her heart jumped to see him look so insecure. She was even more pleased when at the surprise on his face when she shut the door behind her.

He cleared his throat.

"What brings you here?"

She gave him a disdainful look.

"I work here, remember? I thought that you were the one ogling my legs at the marketing meeting. Thanks for inviting me. I really like to see what the other departments are doing."

"Thanks. I have a good staff."

"I didn't realize you were in charge"

His look started to shift from confusion to frustration. Time to change tactics.

"Kidding. You must be a good leader to inspire such good work." She used these words to work him back into the corner. She reached over his head to get the binder clips. She felt him take in a breath when she leaned over him. She didn't have to look to see if he was watching her. She took a step forward, knowing that this would put her breast practically in his face. As she pulled her arm down, clips in hand, she trailed her fingers down the side of his face. She didn't back away. She was standing so close to him that she could smell his skin. The sheer closeness of him and the power she knew she had over him thrilled her. She clenched her thighs together. She drifted her fingers down his chest. She whispered in his ear.

"You don't remember me, do you?"

"Uh. . . No. I'm sorry."

She fought the urge to nibble his earlobe. She breathed into his ear softly and moaned a pre-orgasmic moan.

"Think about it. You will."

With that she turned and walked out, looking back to see his surprised look and the unmistakable bulge in his pants. She was so turned on she didn't even bother to go back to her office. If he came to see her, she wouldn't be able to turn him away. She dashed to the lady's room. No one was in there. Her heart was beating hard as she locked the stall door. She unfastened her pants and slipped her hand into her panties. She was wet and she could feel her clit throbbing before her fingers even touched it. She gave it a few firm strokes and the wetness grew. She rested her head against the cool side of the stall. She massaged her clit rapidly with a practiced touch. It took less than a minute for her to have a mind-blowing orgasm. She bit her lip to keep from moaning out loud. She heard high heels click their way into the room. She hurriedly flushed the toilet and refastened her pants.

She washed her hands and smoothed her hair back. She noticed that her face glowed with a post-orgasmic flush. The look was becoming. She firmly resolved to have more orgasms. She wasn't sure how long she could maintain her chilly demeanor around Tony. She needed someone or something to help relieve this pressure.

She spent the rest of the day leaning forward in her chair so she could feel the seam of her pants pushing against her engorged clit. When her day finally ended, she raced home, ignored the cat, and dug around her closet for the "Gag" gift her sister had given her for Christmas. She had never used it, but all afternoon she thought about the vibrator still snugly wrapped in its box. She went into the bedroom and stripped off her clothes. Her panties were soaked. She was even more excited when she realized that the smell of passion in the room was coming from her. She lay back on her pillows and spread her legs. She used the tip of the vibrator to trace her lips, slowly and softly teasing herself. She used her other hand to part her engorged, turgid lips. She was surprised by the heat coming from her. She stroked and touched herself, sighing and moaning. She dipped the tip of the vibrator into her waiting vagina. It slid in effortlessly. She toyed with herself as she teased it in and out, just an inch at a time. The other hand stroked her clit softly and she flicked it with her fingers. She could feel the pressure building in her loins. She was enjoying this as much as the orgasm she knew was coming. Finally, she couldn't take it anymore and she rammed the vibe into herself. She gave a loud gasp then pulled it back out all the way, then thrust it back in. Then all the way out and in about halfway. Then she tried short strokes, alternating those with deep ones. Finally, she rested the tip about an inch inside and then flipped the switch on.

She came so hard the vibrator moved by itself. She stroked her clit softly as she moved the vibe slowly, feeling tiny tremors rippling through her. She felt completely relaxed.

She was ready for the next day. Maybe, just maybe she would get a little closer to her ultimate revenge.

CHAPTER 2

ANTHONY

NO ONE WAS MORE surprised than Anthony when he got hired for a position with a big company. He had majored in Business and somehow had managed to use his intense charm and general amiability into a fairly lucrative career.

While he enjoyed a small amount of fame in school as a star athlete, he didn't fool himself into thinking that he had a future in professional sports. He knew he paid more attention to partying than to his grades and that he barely got into college. Once he got there, he worked hard, pledging a fraternity only to make future contacts and really focused on doing well. Since none of the other freshmen, at least his fellow pledges, seemed to be doing any work, he rose to the top of his class, making the dean's list both semesters of the first year. It became very clear that the only future he had was of his own making. He worked part-time all summer and attended the summer sessions and was one of the very few members of his fraternity to actually graduate in four years. He immediately applied for an internship with a marketing firm that was only too glad to refer him for the position at this company. He was very young, only twenty-five, but he knew that he would do well. This confidence helped him rise up the ladder to vice-president of marketing by the time he was thirty. The only reason he wasn't president was that the man hadn't retired yet.

He had focused so hard on school and work that outside of a few fraternity parties he hadn't dated anyone since graduating from high school. He didn't have time to invest in anything besides a casual hook-up and even those were few and far between. It didn't matter, he certainly made the most of the opportunities. Casual sex was everywhere. It only took a few quickies in dorm rooms and at parties to make him realize that he wanted more, much more.

Now that he had a little time to breathe and money to spend, he certainly was open to dating. He was walking down the hall on his way to a meeting and he stopped dead in his tracks. There was a tall, slim woman he had never seen before, going through the first day on the job routine. He had no idea whose department she was in. She didn't have that over-processed look of the women in his department, nor did she have the polished sheen of the receptionists. Who was she?

Over the next day, he couldn't shake the feeling that he had seen her before. He didn't know where, but he could kick himself for not remembering. He took a long look at her. Her legs seemed to go on forever and her strawberry blonde hair was the kind of color he knew was natural. He shivered at the thought of seeing her hair loose around her bare shoulders. He was thinking this when she looked straight into his eyes. Her eyes were a deep blue-green and he thought he could drown in them.

He knew that he would do whatever it took to get to know this woman better.

She didn't respond to his charm; in fact, she was barely

civil to him. He thought that he felt some tension and heat between them for a moment in her office. Her chilly demeanor did nothing to deter him. She looked at him and stood so close to him that the electricity between them made the hair on his neck stand on end. He thought that she was going to kiss him, but the phone rang and she dismissed him.

Her cool reaction did nothing to diminish the growing bulge in his pants. He somehow managed to get back to his office and locked himself in, ignoring all of the sly looks the other guys in the department gave him. He was amazed at how well known she became in such a short amount of time. He was even more amazed to discover that she was the new science lab consultant. She certainly didn't look like any of the science people that he had ever encountered before.

Of course, he hadn't really met any scientific types in the last several years. In fact, he didn't really remember knowing anyone who wasn't in his fraternity and before that, on any of his teams.

He had no idea how she would have anything to do with marketing, but he invited her to his group meeting so she could get to know some of the people at the office. He was pleasantly surprised to see the new girl, a woman, actually, sitting near the end of the conference table. She was directly in front of the pull-down screen. This meant that she would be inches away from him. He got a good look at her when she came in. She was wearing a skirt and high heels that made her legs look impossibly long. He couldn't tell you what else she was wearing, all he could see was that skirt and those legs. He had to make a concerted effort to drag his eyes away. He wasn't sure if she was trying to distract him, but if she was, it certainly was working. At one point she dropped her pen and her skirt pulled up when she bent over. He wanted to pick it up for her and stroke her thigh as he handed it back.

That thought was followed by several more. He actually had to stab his hand with his pen so that he would focus. He was grateful for the podium to hide his obvious attraction to her. He was actually sweating by the time the meeting was over.

He even thought about going out to his car to relieve the pressure, but he was pretty sure that would just make things worse. He took every opportunity to walk around just to get the blood flowing to the rest of his body. He walked down to the supply room to get what had to be a year's supply of pens when he heard the door open.

There she was, Brianna, in all of her short-skirted, high-heeled glory. She walked towards him and he couldn't tell if she asked him to get something for her. All could he focus on was how lovely she was. When she stepped into his personal space, he felt like time stood still. He breathed in and smelled a clean lightly floral smell. He immediately got hard. He regretted not going out to his car.

Then she smiled and his focus shifted to her beautiful mouth. Her soft lips just begged to be kissed. He didn't dare move. Then she asked him if he remembered her. The top of his head almost came off when she moaned into his ear. Her hot breath felt so sexy he closed his eyes. The sound of her moan made him weak in the knees.

He didn't know where he knew her from, but he was going to try. Maybe she would make some new memories with him.

He went back to his office and shut the door. He made a list of all the places he could have met her. He knew he hadn't dated her, he certainly would have remembered if she had ever been on his arm at a formal event. So college was out. Maybe she had been a cheerleader for one of the opposing teams he played in high school, but no, a tall girl like that would have stood out. She wasn't the type anyway. Maybe she was a friend of his sister's? He had never been able to single any of them out, so that was a possibility.

Thinking about his sister cooled his passion. He made a mental note to think about his sister the next time he saw Briana.

He didn't have long to wait. His secretary buzzed and said that Brianna wanted to discuss something she thought of at the meeting. Before he could get her to book the conference room, Briana had opened his office door and waltzed in. She didn't even move like normal people. Her long strides took her to his desk. She perched that perfect ass on the edge of his desk. He stood up so fast he knocked several files to the floor.

He bent over to pick them up, his eyes firmly locked on her gorgeous legs. She leaned over the desk, making it very awkward for him to stand up at all, let alone stand up without revealing the bulge in his pants. She cleared her throat and picked up the notepad on his desk. She ticked off the list he had made and then said,

"I was hoping I made a bigger impression on you than that. I'll give you a hint." She hopped off his desk giving him a brief flash of thigh. He stumbled, almost hitting his head on the desk.

"I would have thought Tony the Pistol would move with more grace."

The mention of his old nickname, which he hadn't heard in years, sent a chill over him. He sat down in his chair as she slunk out of his office. He rested his head on his desk for a moment.

He had to know her from high school, but she wasn't a

friend of his sister's. He pulled up the company newsletter introducing the new research consultant. It only took a few moments to get the information he was looking for. As he pored over the list of Brianna's credentials, it slowly started to come together. Science girl from high school, great legs, red hair. He suddenly went pale.

His senior year of high school was just as idyllic as all of his school years had been. It seemed like his wave of popularity was still at its peak. He noticed the one girl in the science club that was working on the Homecoming King float. It was hard not to recognize her. She was the tallest one and her slow, shy smile and clean natural look made her stand out. She was mostly in the background, but he caught her watching him a few times.

He made the rounds to all the parties, not drinking until he got to the last one. The game had really worn him out. He was a little dehydrated and hadn't had time to eat dinner. He was a little light-headed when he got to the party and after one and a half beers, he was on the border between tipsy and drunk. He walked into the kitchen hoping to find some water or maybe some food. The Science girl was leaning against the counter. He took a dizzy look at her and noticed that she was wearing a skirt. Her legs were beautiful. He smiled at her. He didn't remember what he said to her, but soon they were outside on the dark porch. She really listened to him. She didn't prattle on about makeup and shoes and trash the other girls. She was quiet and shy and he was thoroughly charmed by her. He kissed her and her lips were so soft and sweet that he couldn't stop himself. His hands seemed to have a mind of their own as they stroked her soft, sweet skin. He had never felt anything so soft. Her legs were firm and silky. His fingers stroked her over and over. It seemed to make him lose all reason. He was stroking her thigh when his fingers worked their way even further. It wasn't his intention when he started kissing her, but that's where he was and he couldn't stop himself.

His finger slipped inside her glorious wetness and suddenly his goal was making her moan. He kept going, her wetness and clenching thighs told him she was enjoying it. He felt and heard her come at the same time. It was the most intense experience of his life. He went back to stretch his arm before kissing her again, and his arm dropped against her shoulder harder than he intended. He was just about to sit back up when she was unbuttoning his jeans. He was inside her mouth in a matter of seconds and he felt her hot, wet mouth on him. The next thing he knew he had his own mind-blowing orgasm. As soon as he was done, he needed to get something to drink, water, soda, something. He didn't know what to say to her, but he figured that he would have time to figure it out. They could talk when he got back.

Then he was inside and the ridiculous girl who had been Homecoming Queen showed up and insisted that all of her drunk friends take pictures with him. She was very drunk and then she got very sick, all over his shirt. He wound up having to take her home, and then he had to go change. By that time, his parents didn't want him to go back out.

Had Brianna waited all night for him? What did she think when he never came back out? Surely she would have heard about the Queen puking everywhere.

Now he realized that she probably hadn't, she wasn't involved with that crowd. All of these years she must have thought that he had simply walked away after they had been so intimate. And now, when she saw him again, all he could do was ogle her.

He felt like a cad. There was no excuse for behaving the way he had back then. Even if he hadn't made it back to the party, he certainly could have made the effort to talk to her. Now he was older and he still let his hormones push him around.

He would make it up to her. If it was at all possible, he would make amends for his bad behavior and maybe they could start over. All he could do was try.

He spent the rest of the day hiding in his office. Now that he knew what he had done, he didn't want to see her until he found a solution. He spent the rest of the week out of the office, attending to the kind of tasks he usually made the interns do. Over the weekend he thought of a few ways to reach out to Brianna without making a scene. The flowers were too obvious. Any big gesture was sure to be noticed by the office staff. He was certain she would not appreciate that kind of attention.

He finally decided to bring her a plant for her office. He felt stupid doing it, but he needed a reason to talk to her. He dressed carefully that morning, trying to look humble. When he got to work he waited quietly for Briana to arrive. He gave her a few minutes to get settled in her office before he headed that way. Plant in hand, he knocked on her door. He walked right in, leaving the door open, so she wouldn't be too vocal about throwing him out. He set the plant on her desk.

"I wanted to welcome you to the company. . . . I also want to talk to you for a moment. Please, just listen to me for a minute. I do remember you. I'm so, so sorry. I treated you so badly. I really liked you then."

"Then why did you just use me and leave?"

The words sounded so vulnerable and hurt coming from the mouth of such a cool and sophisticated woman.

"I know it must seem that way."

"How else could it seem? That's what happened."

"I didn't mean for things to happen like that. Please give me a chance to explain things to you."

She hesitated and looked him square in the eye. Maybe she saw how sincere he was because she only faltered for a moment.

"All right. Just not here."

They agreed to meet for a late lunch at a small coffee shop nearby.

He was on pins and needles all afternoon. He was shocked by his nervousness. He had been managing large accounts and risking hundreds of thousands of dollars for years, but somehow he felt there was so much more at stake here.

He was too nervous to eat so he arrived early to calm his nerves. He was surprised to see that she was already there. He stumbled a little as he sat down. He couldn't tell if her smile was because she was pleased to see him, or if she was laughing at him for being clumsy. It didn't matter; it was an opening and he would take it.

"Have you ordered?"

"I just want coffee."

He indicated to the waitress to bring him a cup.

"I'm so glad you agreed to meet me."

"I wanted to hear what you have to say after all of these years."

She stared him square in the eye and he blushed. He hoped he could get through this without stammering.

"That night did not turn out how I wanted it to."

"Which part, the making out, the blow job, or the leaving me alone in the yard?"

"The leaving you alone part."

She seemed surprised to hear that

"It was a very strange night. I didn't drink until I got there and by then I was so tired and worn out that the beer made me dizzy. Then I saw you. You were so soft and inno-cent-looking standing there when I came into the kitchen that I couldn't believe that I hadn't really seen you before, so I asked you to go outside. I really just wanted to talk."

"Sure, so why did you kiss me?"

"I couldn't resist you."

"Yeah, I couldn't keep the guys away from me and my hot math club brain."

"You don't understand; it was because you were so different from all the other girls that I couldn't keep from kissing you. Then one thing led to another and I was so lightheaded that I acted without thinking. And then all I wanted to do was to make you feel good."

"Then you wanted me to make you feel good."

"I didn't mean for that to happen. When you started, I didn't want you to stop. And when you finished, I wanted to go inside and bring back some drinks for us so we could talk."

"Right, that's when you decided you needed to leave me out there."

"No, that's not it at all. I got sidetracked by some drunk cheerleaders."

She raised an eyebrow at him and he blushed again.

"That's not what I mean. "

He explained it as best he could. He could see her chilly demeanor start to slip away.

"I'm so sorry. I didn't see you again at any of the parties

or anywhere. I thought you didn't want to speak to me and I was too embarrassed to try and find you. Please, I'm sorry. I was just a stupid kid back then."

"And now . . . ?"

"I'm a slightly less stupid adult."

He placed his hand on top of hers. Her hand was cool and soft. She didn't pull away, and he was encouraged.

"Please, please let me make it up to you?"

For a brief moment, she looked into his eyes and gave him a genuine smile. His heart skipped a beat and there was an electric moment between. It was over much too soon.

She cleared her throat.

"Take me out tonight. Cocktails and..."

"And...?"

"And we'll see if you've done enough."

The rest of the day went by too fast for him to get nervous. He knew that all he could do was try.

She met him downstairs. They made small talk as they walked to a new wine bar close to the office. He started to order for them both when she interrupted.

"Let me." She quickly and expertly ordered a wine and appetizers.

The wine was delicious and paired perfectly. Each taste was exquisite. The warmth of the wine spread across his tongue sensually. The sharp taste of the accompanying cheese was like a light nip on the neck during a slow delicious bout of lovemaking.

He wondered if he were some kind of pervert to think this way during an apology meeting. He felt the warmth of a blush wash over him.

"I never thought that I would see Tony the Pistol blush."

"In high school, I never thought I would get tired of that

nickname. I haven't heard that in years. People called me Anthony in college."

"Which do you prefer?"

"Anthony. I'm not the same person I was back then."

"I'm starting to see that."

He didn't know if she was just stringing him along, but he didn't really care at this point. She was listening. She was so lovely. He wondered what would have happened if he had actually tried to get a hold of her way back then. Would they have dated? Would they still be together?

He didn't have much time to dwell on this. She was finishing her wine.

"I better go."

"Wait... "

He reached out for her hand. She let him take it. His fingers stroked the back of her hand.

"Have I made it up to you?"

"You have made a good start."

He pulled her gently towards him and kissed her softly. Her lips opened to him and they both spilled into a much deeper kiss than either intended.

"I really better go."

She seemed so eager to leave he couldn't do anything but let her go.

He called after her, "Can I see you again?"

He didn't think she heard him. As he waited for the check, he got a message on his phone.

"Yes, you can see me again. I will let you know the details later."

He never thought he would feel so lighthearted about anything, especially not something as vague as a half-promise. Brianna was the only thing he could think about all the way home. He was very hopeful and very horny. Instead of trying to dampen his ardor with a cold shower, he lay back in his bed and thought about Brianna.

He imagined getting a chance to show her how truly lovely he thought she was. Let's see, he would take her away to some romantic setting. Not a beach, he would hate to see her fair skin burn. Maybe a ski resort. He would love to unwrap her from layers of warm clothing and kiss the tips of her fingers until she warmed up.

He wondered if he was going crazy, acting like some infatuated teenager. Could he be falling in love?

He slept, his mind weaving a fascinating dream. He was sitting in a chair next to a warm fire. He could hear it crackling and smell the flames, warm and seductive. He turned and saw Brianna stepping towards him, slim and seductive in a pair of faded jeans, her stomach flat and her bottom curving pleasantly in the snug denim. She was wearing a long-sleeved shirt that was slightly too small. It pulled across her breasts accentuating her tightening nipples. He reached for her and drew her to him. She smiled at him as he pulled her onto his lap. She fit perfectly against him, her long legs draping over the arm of the chair as he kissed her. Her mouth opened and her tongue darted out to meet him. He felt himself falling into her warmth. His hand slipped under the edge of her shirt, stroking the plains of her stomach, feeling the velvety softness of her skin. His hand edged further up. His hand cupped her bare breast. He felt rather than heard her moan under his kiss. His thumb stroked her nipple into a firm, tight peak. Her nipple felt like rough silk and he teased it as she squirmed, rubbing her rump against him. She stood and pulled her shirt over her head, her breasts gloriously free. He opened his arms and she stepped into them. He leaned forward and licked her nipples, feeling her shudder of pleasure. He held one breast in his hand as he thoroughly worshipped the other. He thrilled to the sound of her moan and he cupped her bottom and pulled her to him. He was just about to twirl his tongue in her navel when he heard a loud shrieking alarm.

With that, he woke up, covered in sweat. His hands were still cupped as if on Brianna's firm butt.

He could not wait to get to work and see what she had to say to him today.

He didn't see her when he came in, but she must have been there. There was a mug of coffee waiting on his desk for him. It sat squarely in the center holding a note in place. It said simply, "My office, 12:15 -B"

He knew that she picked this time because most people would either be out for lunch at 12 or already back from an early meal. 12:15 was perfect because it was when the building was at its quietest.

He was not at all prepared for what he saw when she let him in. She was wearing the tightest, shortest skirt possible. She was wearing high heels which made her exactly the same height as him. Her shirt was tailored so well that it was like a second skin. Even buttoned all the way up it was sexier than any slinky piece of lingerie. As soon as the door clicked shut behind him she had her hands planted firmly on his ass. She pulled him against her and ground her pelvis into him. He got so hard so fast he was surprised he didn't pass out. She pressed him to her as she took his hands and placed them on her breasts. He was too surprised to do anything other than kiss her back when she kissed him. His hands wandered over to the buttons on her shirt. Very, very carefully he undid each button. He let his thumbs stroke her skin, feeling the soft warmth as her skin was revealed. Her shirt fell open revealing a lacy beige bra. Her breasts were held up perkily as if she was offering them to him. He wanted to bury his face in them, but he let her lead his hands to her skirt. Instead of pushing them around to her waistband, she pushed them under her skirt. He felt the silky tops of her stockings, then the soft skin of her inner thighs. He slipped his hands around to cup her ass as he had in his dream. He was pleasantly surprised to feel her bare skin.

He didn't think it was possible to grow any harder. He softly caressed her as she kissed him hungrily. The harder he kissed her, the softer his touch became. He was lightly tracing her ass when she pressed against him. She bit his lip and practically growled, "Fuck Me, Tony."

He gently lifted her up and carried her to the edge of her desk. She leaned back and her breasts bobbled fetchingly at him. He kept himself from nibbling her. She pulled her skirt all the way up, spreading her legs wantonly. He leaned over her and kissed her even softer than before. She moaned impatiently and reached for his crotch, fumbling at the waistband of his pants. He unfastened them for her and she tugged the down. He felt them slide to his knees. She arched her back and looked him in the eye. He could see that they were dark with lust.

That broke any resolve he may have had. With one quick movement, he had his boxers off. He reached for her legs and pulled her down to the edge of the desk. She reached behind her and handed him a condom. He made quick work of putting it on.

She was so wet and ready for him that he slipped inside of her as if she had been custom made for him. The minute he was inside her all the way, she locked her legs around his hips. She undulated under him as he slowly moved in and out, relishing each thrust and enjoying the feel of her beneath him. She made a noise of impatience and began to buck under him.

"Come on, Tony. Fuck me!"

He didn't expect this at all. He wasn't sure if she was really overcome with lust for him or if she was playing some kind of game. After a few moments, he didn't care. He gripped the desk beneath him and began to drive into her with a strong steady beat. He heard her moan of pleasure as his thrust went deeper and became faster. She arched her back underneath him and he began plunging in short hard strokes. She tensed her thighs around him. He thrust hard and firm inside her and felt her tense up around him and under him. He felt her come in short sharp waves. She was still clenching around him when the phone rang from the corner. He leaned forward and looked over.

"Is your top line for the Big Boss?"

"Yes."

"That's them on the phone."

He pulled out of her, unsatisfied as she pulled her shirt back around her. She sat up and tugged her skirt down as she reached for the phone. She motioned for him to go as she reached for a pen.

He knew enough by now not to lose contact with her. He had blown one chance to be with her, he wasn't going to let her get away from him again.

CHAPTER 3

TOGETHER AT LAST

BRIANNA RUSHED THROUGH HER AFTERNOON. She wanted a moment or two to relish in the afterglow of what had been the ultimate revenge. She had asked her secretary to call her at precisely 12:35 from the executive conference room. Her plan had almost been foiled by Anthony's insistence at savoring the moment. Still, it had turned out the way she wanted. She got a nice, satisfactory orgasm and he was left wanting more. The next step in her plan was to ignore him completely.

The only problem was that she wasn't sure she could do it.

She found herself smiling all afternoon and into the evening. When she got home, she couldn't bring herself to shower off the scent of him. She preferred to bask in the smell of him on her skin. Her lips were slightly bruised from the kissing and her body ached pleasantly from Anthony's hard thrusts. She told herself that was all it was, that what she was feeling was the ripples from a nice hard fuck. If she told herself that enough, it might even be true.

She spent the next morning in the lab so she didn't get

to see the cup of coffee and the freshly baked cookie until that afternoon. She smiled. He had done his research and found out that she loved shortbread. She sniffed the cold coffee. It was a dark French roast. It had probably been delicious when it was hot. It wasn't his fault that she hadn't been there to get it. She found herself caring that he thought she hadn't bothered to thank him. She picked up the phone and dialed his extension only to discover that he was out for the afternoon. She decided to do some research of her own.

She typed in his last name before she realized she was in the wrong database. By the time she realized her mistake, the page had loaded. She leaned forward and squinted at the screen. A few more keystrokes and she had some very interesting information. By the time she was finished reading, she discovered that she had also behaved badly and that Tony wasn't the heel she thought he was all these years.

The afternoon passed too slowly. She knew that she had to wait until after six or maybe even later to call him, but she was getting impatient. At exactly six-thirty, she picked up her cell phone and dialed Tony's number. He answered before it immediately.

"I was just about to call you."

"Oh? Well, I could hang up if you still want to."

He laughed a rich laugh that made a tingle run all the way down her spine, reminding her of how he had made her feel.

"I'm sorry I didn't call to thank you for the coffee."

"I'm sorry you didn't get it when it was hot."

She wanted to make a sexually charged remark but thought better of it.

"Can we meet later this evening?"

"I'm with a client until 8, but after is good, if it's not too late for you."

"It's not."

She gave him her address and hung up the phone. She was hoping it wasn't too late for them.

She filled the time by selecting wine and arranging her living room into the perfect setting for seduction. She arranged the bed to be equally inviting. She took a warm, scented bath; afterward, she rubbed her skin with lush-smelling almond oil. It felt delicious on her skin. She massaged it in, feeling the soft curve of her calves. She rubbed it into her thighs, rubbing the muscles with her fingers. She pressed her thumbs along the strong muscles of her inner things. She propped her leg up on the bathroom counter and rubbed the oil into the firm flesh of her buttocks. She gave a little moan and she traced the lips of her pussy from behind. She was hot and wet. She was more than ready for him. But she had time for an appetizer. She turned and took inventory of her body in the mirror. Her stomach was lean, but there was a little bit of a womanly curve. Her buttocks were also delightfully curvy. She admired the dip at her lower back and the way her waist nipped in and softly led her eye to her breasts. She used to wish they were larger, but now she was happy with the way they were. Her hands cupped each breast and she watched the nipple get harder under her gaze. She tweaked each one and felt the electric charge rush through her body to her pussy. She glanced at the clock. He would be here soon. She rubbed her hand across her breasts and gave her bottom a light spank. She would have to wait.

She pulled on a pair of silk pajamas over her bare skin and waited.

He didn't make her wait long.

The doorbell rang and she walked languidly to answer. She showed him in and he smiled at her, taking in the low light of the room. She looked relaxed and beautiful bathed in the soft light, her hair down, her body lightly kissed by the silk.

She led him in and offered him a glass of wine. He sat on the sofa and she sat next to him. She turned toward him and the cat sauntered over and gave him a sniff. He reached out and absently scratched the cat's ears. Satisfied, the cat wandered away. Brianna smiled.

"You have a lovely smile."

"Thank you."

"I hope I have given you something to smile about."

"You have, but I don't really have the right to accept them."

His brow furrowed and he looked at her curiously.

He was about to speak and she stilled his question with a touch on his lips.

"I want to apologize to you, Anthony. All of these years, and most of yesterday I thought you were still the shallow, pompous jock you were in high school. Maybe you weren't even what I thought you were back then.

"I wish I had been less focused on myself. Back then I was so encumbered by own low self-esteem that I couldn't see things very clearly. I thought I wasn't good enough for you, so I bottled myself up and couldn't fathom the idea of someone like you wanting someone like me. No, wait, let me finish. You didn't see me much after that night, because I made sure to stay far away from you.

"When I saw you again and saw how you looked at me, I thought maybe now I could get my revenge. I wanted to make you want me. I could have you briefly, take my satisfaction and then leave you cold and lonely. I really wanted to do that.

"But I can't get away from how I feel. Seeing you again,

I thought maybe the feeling was just an unrequited crush. But it's not. When I saw the coffee and the cookie, I realized that you aren't the person I thought you were...I know about your sister."

The color drained from his face and he looked incredibly uncomfortable.

"I know that she got very sick, very quickly and that no one knew what it was or what to do. I know that your family got her in one of our drug trials. She was one of the few that it helped. I know that you started working for the company immediately after school because you were so pleased with the results of the study."

"It saved my sister's life. This company held my family together."

He had tears in his eyes and she felt a twinge in her heart. She couldn't help herself. She leaned forward and kissed his lips softly. She put her hand on his shoulder and leaned forward to kiss the corner of his eye. She kissed his face, and his nose then backs down to his lips. She kissed him until his mouth relaxed.

"You are not the boy I thought you were. You are the man I thought I would never meet."

He wrapped his arms around her and caught her in an enormous hug. He pulled her forward and she landed on his lap. Her silk pajamas were so slick she almost slid off. They laughed when he caught her.

She stood up and held her hand out to him. He took it and she led him to the bedroom.

She sat on the edge of the bed and drew him to her. She slowly unbuttoned his shirt; her touch was gentle. The crispy starched shirt opened to reveal a white undershirt. She removed the shirt and tugged the undershirt off over his head. His chest was firm and lightly sprinkled with hair. He was lean and muscular. Over the years, he had maintained his athlete's build. She licked his nipple and then gave it a light nip. She inhaled deeply, absorbing his scent. She licked her way down to his stomach. Her hand slipped down to stroke this ass through his trousers. He moaned. She saw and felt the bulge in his pants grow. She unfastened his pants and slipped her hand into the opening. Her hand felt the soft fabric of his boxer shorts she gave a tug and the shorts and pants slid to the ground. His beautiful penis sprang forward. It was as pleasingly beautiful as the rest of him. She reached for him and stroked him softly. She leaned forward and gave the head a lick. She wrapped her tongue around him like he was her favorite flavor of ice cream.

She heard him say in a gruff voice, "You're going to make me fall down."

"Can't have that."

She drew him down on the bed and climbed on top of him moving in between his legs and scooting down. She looked at him for a long moment and then continued to lick him. She thoroughly laved the head, and then flicked her tongue across the top. She held him firmly in one hand as she opened her mouth to take him in all the way. He gasped. She sucked him in and slid him out. She alternated the slow, deep sucks with light flickering licks. She cupped his balls lightly in one hand as she worked. She could hear his sighs and moans.

He nudged at her shoulders and she looked up at him.

"I don't want this to end too soon."

He tugged her upwards and she lay beside him. He moved to make room for her then suddenly he was on top of her. He knelt between her legs and placed his hand on her stomach. He rubbed slow, steady circles on the silk, it rubbed against her delightfully. He leaned forward and kissed her softly. His hand dipped under the edge of her top. It worked its way up to her breast and she almost wept in gratitude as he cupped it and teased her waiting nipple by rubbing it with his thumb. His hand darted back down and he sat up.

He slowly unbuttoned the top, opening it to reveal her glorious flesh. He dipped his head and twirled his tongue on the tip of her nipple, then licking it. He switched back and forth between the two until they were each so hard they almost ached. Then he sucked on them. Her body grew tense and he began to lick his way down towards her stomach. He pulled the pants down slowly so her mound revealed itself to him. He didn't pull them down all the way, just enough to dip the tip of his tongue between the lips of her pussy. He timed his exploration perfectly to the removal of her bottoms. They slipped luxuriously off and he discarded them. He blew lightly on her lips and she sighed. He parted her legs gently and began flicking her clit with the tip of his tongue. He heard a sharp intake of breath, but he didn't stop his relentless flicking. He felt her grow wet under the tip of his tongue and gloried in the smell of her. Just when she thought she couldn't stand it anymore, he began to lick at her with strong deliberate licks of his whole tongue. She moaned and spread her legs. He moved down and draped one of her long, lovely legs over each shoulder. He licked her from the opening of her vagina to the tip of her clit. He tasted every drop as it formed. She grew wetter and wetter. She began to rotate her hips and he increased the pressure of his tongue. He moved his hands up. He slid one under her to cup and knead her buttocks. He took advantage of her wide, open wetness and slowly entered her with one finger, then two. Her moans grew louder. He licked and moved fingers at the same rhythm. He felt her hips tense up underneath his lips. He stopped licking her and began sucking on her clit relentlessly. She came with sharp sound and flooded his mouth with her juices. He returned to licking her as she still jerked her hips forward. His licks grew softer as she recovered from the strong, intense orgasm. He licked his way back up her stomach as her body relaxed and her legs drifted down from his shoulders. He kissed all the way back up to her neck and kissed her mouth softly. She moaned again.

"I can taste myself on your lips."

He smiled.

"Are you ready for me?"

"You have no idea."

He crawled down and fumbled in his pants. He slipped on the condom with a speed that surprised her. He dipped his head again and gave her a long lingering lick. She parted her legs and he entered her slowly, draping her legs around his hips. He moved so slowly she felt every heavenly inch as he went inside her. When he was all the way in, he pulled back out just as slowly. She never thought the thrill of anticipation would give so much to the act itself. His slow, exact movements seemed to penetrate her very soul.

He moved slowly and deeply and her body began a slow burn that she knew was going to turn into a delicious tingle. She took a deep breath and just enjoyed the feel of him moving inside her. She was delightfully wet and he began to give his hips a little grind as he moved in and out. She moved back at him and he increased his pace. Soon they were both grinding against each other as he moved faster and faster. She began to moan with each thrust. Her sounds seemed to spur him on She knew he could bring her pleasure with sharp, deep thrusting. She didn't know she could get a stronger, more intense pleasure with equally deep, but much softer thrusts.

They built up a mutually pleasing pace. She moaned and sighed and felt him deeper and deeper. He sped up and she met him thrust for thrust. They rocked together and she felt another orgasm build deep inside her. This one was going to be even deeper than the first. Suddenly, almost without warning, the orgasm broke in sharp, bright waves. It churned deep inside her. He felt her muscles tense around him and he felt every ripple. He couldn't hold himself back any longer. He gave two slower, deep thrusts before his orgasm burst through him. It seemed to come from his entire body. Brianna wrapped around him as they both subsided. She sighed as they relaxed into each other.

Spent, tired they lay still for a long, long moment.

Brianna smiled at him.

"Anthony, that was fantastic."

"Brianna, it was beyond fantastic."

"This isn't just an affair, is it?"

"No, it's not."

"We fit together so perfectly."

"You don't have to convince me. "

"No, but I could try."

She gave him a devilish look and pushed him over onto his back. She nuzzled his neck and reached down to remove the condom. She skipped lightly out of bed to take care of it. She bounced back to bed as he watched the fetching sight of her breasts bobbling. She climbed on top of him and licked him delicately on the tip of his earlobe. She savored the slightly salty taste of his skin as she worked her way across his jaw and down to his throat. Her long hair draped over him as she licked him. She inhaled deeply, finding his smell incredibly arousing. He sighed underneath her. She wanted to make him moan with pleasure. She reached his pelvic area and began to mouth his hipbones. She nuzzled his flat stomach with her cheek. He reached out and stroked her hair. She ran her tongue down the length of his cock and it twitched slightly. She smiled and mouthed her way down his thigh. She switched to the other leg and worked her way back up. By the time she got back to his waist, his cock was standing up to greet her. She was never one to refuse a polite invitation so she opened her mouth and took as much of him in as she could at once. She drew in a deep breath and took a long, slow suck.

He moaned loudly. She held him firmly in one hand and slid her mouth up and down, getting into a slow and steady rhythm. He sighed and she continued, this time adding a light lick with the flat of her tongue. She slowed down and timed the licks with the sounds of his moans. She stopped for a moment and worked her way back up to his chest. He opened his arms for her and she curled up into them, letting her hand drift lazily down to stroke his cock. He tipped her mouth up to his and he gave her a long, slow kiss. They melted into each other and she continued her strong firm strokes on him.

It wasn't enough. She stopped stroking and he made a frustrated sound. She leaned across him to her nightstand and he gave her bare bottom a light spank that sent a thrill through her entire body. She returned to him and slowly slid the condom over him. She held him with one hand and then gathered herself up and climbed on top of him. She gave a slight gasp as he slid in. She closed her eyes as she began to ride him. She rose up and slid down, working her rhythm in time with his sighs and moans. His hands reached up to clutch her hips. She moved up and down and felt yet another orgasm building. She climbed off and turned around. Facing his feet she slid back down on top of him. He patted her ass in approval as he felt himself go into her even deeper than before. She leaned forward and moved up and down.

His hand rested on her back and he stroked the top of her buttocks as she moved up and down. This angle made his cock rubbed against her g-spot while his balls tickled her clit. The feeling was so delicious she didn't want it to ever end. She rose and fell and ground around. The pleasure began to build deep inside her. She began to speed up and he squeezed her ass firmly. She was working herself up into a frenzy. She held onto his ankles for support as she moved back forth. She finally gripped onto to him and came so hard and so intensely she thought she may have lost consciousness for a moment. She climbed up and nestled next to him.

"Why is it that every time I try to please you, it turns into a mind-blowing orgasm for me?"

"Is that a problem?"

"No, not at all, but I want you to get something out of it, too."

She looked so intent and concerned that all he could do was kiss her.

"Trust me, this is exactly where I want to be."

They kissed and cuddled until they both fell asleep.

ABOUT THE AUTHOR

Heather Stolts is an emerging erotica author of many erotica kinks and sub-genres. Be sure to check out other books and leave a review if this story got you hot!

Visit my blog at Heather Stolts Blog

Join my newsletter for exclusive previews Heather Stolts Newsletter

Sign up for Free Stories from Xplicit Press Authors

Xplicit Press Author Updates

Like Xplicit Press on Facebook

Follow Xplicit Press on Twitter

Readers: I want to expand a few of the stories to see where the characters can be explored further. If there are any of the stories that you would like to read more about again, I'd love to hear from you!

Keep In Touch
Heather Stolts
info@heatherstolts.com